Four Happy Teletubbies

BBC

One day in Teletubbyland,

all the Teletubbies were feeling very, very happy.

Four happy Teletubbies jumping round a tree.

Happy Teletubbies!

One jumped away

Jumpy, jumpy, jump!

and then there were ...

three!

Three happy Teletubbies.
What did they do?

One went to hide

and then there were ...

two!

Two happy
Teletubbies out
for a run.

Faster and faster

and then there was ...

one!

One happy
Teletubby sitting
in the sun ...

rolled right away

and then there were ...

none!

Where have all the Teletubbies gone?

One happy Teletubby playing peek-a-boo!

Along came another

and then there were ...

two!

Look!
Dipsy's hat!

Look!

Two happy
Teletubbies.
What did
they see?

They saw another Teletubby

and then there were ...

three!

Three happy Teletubbies.
Are there any more?

Of course there are

so then there were ...

four!

 **One!**

 **Two!**

 **Three!**

 **Four!**

Four happy Teletubbies.
What a happy game and Teletubbies
want to play again and again.

Teletubbies love each other very much.

Dipsy Dances

One day in Teletubbyland,
Dipsy was dancing.

B-ptum,
b-ptum,
b-ptum!

Along came Laa-Laa with her ball...

Laa-Laa wanted Dipsy to play with the ball.

And Dipsy danced!

Tinky Winky wanted Dipsy
to play marching.

Dipsy play
marching?

Um ... er...

But Dipsy wanted
to dance.

Dipsy
dance.

Owww!
Bye bye Dipsy!

Bye bye
Tinky Winky!

And Dipsy danced!

Along came Po on her scooter.

Po wanted Dipsy to play rolling.

Po rolled down the hill.

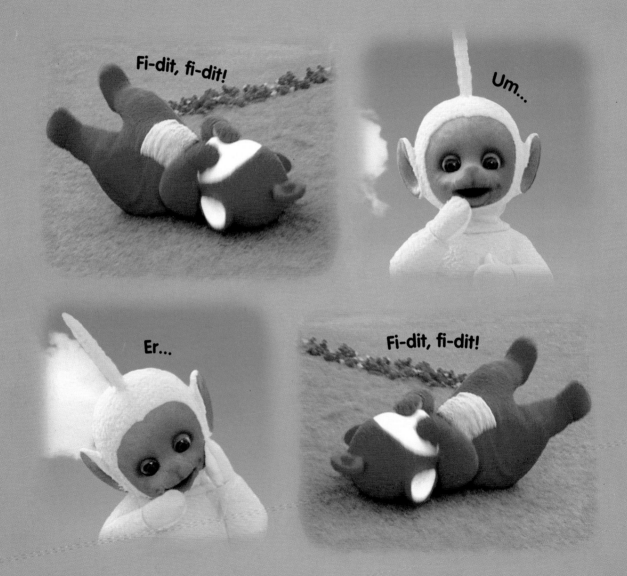

But Dipsy wanted to dance.

And Dipsy danced!

Laa-Laa played with her ball.

Tinky Winky played marching.

Po played rolling ...

and Dipsy danced!

Tinky Winky, Laa-Laa and Po danced.

Everyone danced!
Teletubbies love dancing ...

and Teletubbies love each other very much!

Original paperback editions of *Four Happy Teletubbies* and *Dipsy Dances*
first published in 1998 by BBC Worldwide Ltd, Woodlands, 80 Wood Lane, London WI2 0TT
This hardback edition © 2000 BBC Worldwide Ltd
From original TV scripts by Andrew Davenport
Digiframes™ by Screenscene Ltd
Design make-up by The Dirty Cat Design Partnership
Text, design and illustrations © BBC Worldwide Ltd
Teletubbies charcters and logo © 1996 Ragdoll Limited
Printed and bound in Singapore.

ISBN 0 563 47537 4